Hairy Maclary's SHOWBUSINESS

Lynley Dodd

Gareth Stevens Children's Books
MILWAUKEE

In Riverside Hall
on Cabbage Tree Row,
the Cat Club was having
its Annual Show.

There were fat cats
and thin cats,
tabbies and grays,
kick-up-a-din cats
with boisterous ways.
Cooped up in cages,
they practiced their wails
while their owners fussed over
their teeth
and their
tails.

Out in the street,
tied to a tree,
Hairy Maclary
was trying to see.
He struggled and squirmed,
he unraveled the knot,
and dragging his lead,
he was off
at the
trot.

He bounced up the steps,
he pounced through the door,
he pricked up his ears,
and he pranced round the floor;
flapping and flustering,
bothering,
blustering,
leaving behind him
a hiss
and a
roar.

"STOP!"
cried the President,
"COLLAR HIM, QUICK!"
But Hairy Maclary
was slippery slick.

He slid under tables,

13

he jumped over chairs,

15

he skittered through legs,

and he sped down the stairs.

19

In and out doorways,
through banners and flags,

tangling together
belongings and bags.

Along came Miss Plum
with a big silver cup.
"GOT HIM!" she said
as she snaffled him up.

Preening and purring,
the prizewinners sat
with their rosettes and cups
on the prizewinners' mat . . .

and WHO
won the prize
for the SCRUFFIEST CAT?

Hairy Maclary
from Donaldson's Dairy.

For a free color catalog describing Gareth Stevens' list
of high-quality children's books, call 1-800-341-3569 (USA)
or 1-800-461-9120 (Canada).

GOLD STAR FIRST READERS

Picnic Pandemonium by M. Christine Butler

HELP! by Nigel Crosser

and by Lynley Dodd...

Hairy Maclary from Donaldson's Dairy
Hairy Maclary Scattercat
Hairy Maclary's Bone
Hairy Maclary's Caterwaul Caper
Hairy Maclary's Rumpus at the Vet
The Apple Tree

A Dragon in a Wagon
Find Me a Tiger
Slinky Malinki
The Smallest Turtle
Wake Up, Bear

Library of Congress Cataloging-in-Publication Data

Dodd, Lynley
    Hairy Maclary's showbusiness / by Lynley Dodd. -- North American ed.
      p. cm. -- (Gold star first readers)
    Summary: Fur rises and havoc ensues when Hairy Maclary the dog intrudes upon a cat show.
    ISBN 0-8368-0763-4
    [1. Dogs--Fiction. 2 Cats--Fiction. 3. Stories in rhyme.] I. Title. II. Series.
    PZ8.3.D637Hap   1992
    [E]--dc20   91-50554

North American edition first published in 1992 by
Gareth Stevens Children's Books
1555 North RiverCenter Drive, Suite 201
Milwaukee, Wisconsin 53212, USA

First published in New Zealand by Mallinson Rendel Publishers Ltd.
Copyright © 1991 by Lynley Dodd

Printed in MEXICO.

1 2 3 4 5 6 7 8 9 97 96 95 94 93 92